Air Magic

Mark Jeffrey Stefik

Illustrated by Mark & Barbara Stefik

The Oberlanders: Book 8

The Oberlanders

Published by Portola Publishing
Portola Valley, Ca. 94028 USA

© 2021 by Mark Jeffrey Stefik

Illustrations for the book are by Mark Jeffrey Stefik and Barbara Stefik.

Air Magic the eighth book in *The Oberlanders*. The books describe fictional events in a universe including the planets Sol #3 and Zorcon.

Further information about the series can be found at www.PortolaPublishing.com

Library of Congress Cataloging-in-Publication Data
Copyright Office Registration Number:
Stefik, Mark Jeffrey
    Air Magic / Mark Jeffrey Stefik
Edition 4
ISBN: 978-1-943176-18-2

Sol #3 seemed to be a remote and backwards planet. Nothing ever happened there that would be dangerous for Zorcon's space traveling civilization. Then anomalies started appearing including things that resembled fairy tales. Zorcon's computing and power grids crashed, and an android went rogue. Oversight, Zorcon's powerful security agency, became alarmed. It sent an expedition to investigate. When its starship emerged from a wormhole, it collided with asteroids that should not be there. Meanwhile on Sol #3, Cinderwan was just completing her Elder training in the Water Element when Moriah the Ancient decided to test her. Handling the asteroid crisis would be a worthy challenge. Never mind that succeeding would require skills beyond those of any living Elder.

Air Magic

Books in *The Oberlanders*

The Sendroids series continues after *The Oberlanders*. Information about both series can be found on the website www.PortolaPublishing.com

Air Magic

ACKNOWLEDGMENTS

Thank you to our wonderful friends and early readers who read earlier versions of the folktales of *The Oberlanders* as we developed them. Special thanks to Asli Aydin, Phil Berghausen, Eric and Emma Bier, Danny Bobrow, J.J. and Stu Card, Nilesh and Laura Doctor, Ollie Eggiman, Lance Good, Craig Heberer, Chris Kavert, Ray and Lois Kuntz, Raj and Zoe Minhas, Ranjeeta Prakash, Mary Ann Puppo, Jamie Richard, Lynne Russell, Mali Sarpangal, Jackie Shek, Morgan Stefik, Sebastian Steiger, Frank Torres, Paige Turner, Blanca Vargas, Barry and Joyce Vissell, Alan and Pam Wu, Meili Xu, and their kids and young relatives.

Thank you also to the people of Gimmelwald and Mürren, Switzerland in the Swiss Alps and the people of Vetan in Valle d'Aosta in the Italian Alps. These places inspired us with their natural beauty and stillness, and the power of the mountains, lakes, forests, and waterfalls. The people of the Alps have histories and traditions that reach back into legend and folktale.

Air Magic

CONTENTS

Air Magic

"Why study physics? That's what the computers are for!" Transcript of testimony of Marie Gottmothercus from the *Inquiry into the Ski Mountain Incident*. Declassified Archives of the Zorcon Empire.

Air Magic

1 Breakfast at the North Pole

*H*i there, Fairy Godmother!" Marie Gottmothercus looked up from her table outside Borrones Inn in Santa's Village. Goldilocks, James, and Luke walked towards her.

"Hi there, Fairy Godmother!"

The Fairy Godmother nodded to the young Turner elves. "Hello again, James and Goldilocks. Good morning, Luke."

James and Luke made toys in Nick's workshop. James had flown Mary Ellen and the Fairy Godmother to the North Pole in Santa's sleigh.

Marie could have reassembled her landing craft.

Unlike Zorcon, Sol #3 had no long-distance public transportation. Although Sol #3 natives sometimes rode astride their dragon friends, Marie was not interested in riding on a dragon. For her, Santa's sleigh was the only way to fly. It was much more exhilarating than the trains and sky capsules of Zorcon.

At the start of her mission to Sol #3, Marie had flown her landing craft down from her starship. Marie could have reassembled the landing craft for this trip to the North Pole. But buzzing around Sol #3 in a "bubble" would attract attention. The Department of Planetary Anthropology on Zorcon was fussy about showing natives any advanced technology. The rule of the three L's required that planetary anthropologists "Listen, Learn, and Leave it alone."

Marie could have reassembled her landing craft.

Even creating Santa's flying sleigh had caused problems for Marie with Zorcon University. It wasn't fair. The flying sleigh was Cinderella's idea. Marie had helped to keep it reasonable. For some reason, a supersonic sled pulled by flying reindeer was not seen as reasonable by the powers that be. She smiled at her mischievous thinking. The sleigh was pretty cool, though.

Her professors also did not like that Cinderella was using her Glass Slippers to control Zorcon technology. Again, that wasn't Marie's fault. Cyber safeguards were supposed to prevent such things. Fixing faulty cybernetic technology was not her job. That had not been included in her training.

If anthropology courses didn't cover something important, that also wasn't Marie's fault. Professor Grimmicus was the chairman of the Department of Planetary Anthropology. Curriculum design was his responsibility. She sighed.

"Toy making is great, but there is nothing else to do here."

"How are the new toys coming along?" Marie asked James, Luke and Goldilocks as they approached.

"The new designs and toys are coming along fine," answered James.

"But the elves are getting restless," added Luke.

Goldilocks looked to her brothers. "The toymakers have been living and working at the North Pole for a long time," she explained to the Fairy Godmother. "Toy making is great, but there is nothing else for them to do here."

Goldilocks pointed at the sun resting low in the sky. "The sun has been 'rising' now for several weeks. The bizarre daylight cycle at the North Pole does not help with morale."

"Summer is coming," observed James. "Then there will be 180 days of daylight!"

"And then six more months of pure darkness," moaned Luke.

The Fairy Godmother nodded. "Nature can be so inconvenient," she mused.

"Nature can be so inconvenient."

When the Zorconians decided to build a city at their planet's North Pole, they adjusted the daylight cycle and the polar climate. Space-based reflectors redirected sunlight and provided a more familiar 24-hour cycle of daytime and nighttime at the poles. They also installed heating pipes to warm the neighborhoods in their polar city.

"Any word on the Ski Mountain?" asked James.

"I will have something to show you in a few days," answered the Fairy Godmother. Marie thought about the commands she had given her wand to bring an asteroid to Sol #3. She smiled as she sipped her cinnamon tea and munched on a morning bun. She continued, "Good cooking takes time!"

Goldilocks had seen the new girl at the cottage window.

Goldilocks laughed quietly to herself as the Fairy Godmother talked about good cooking. No one had ever seen the Fairy Godmother cook anything. Now she had a girl to cook for her and help around the cottage. Goldilocks had seen the new girl at the cottage window when they left for the North Pole. She had not met her yet.

Goldilocks sold real estate. She was interested in the business opportunities of a Ski Mountain in Oberland Kingdom. Looking to the Fairy Godmother, she said, "If you put a ski mountain in Oberland Kingdom, I have an idea for its name."

Marie raised an eyebrow and waited.

"The Matterhorn," smiled Goldilocks.

The Fairy Godmother beamed. "Matterhorn" sounded like "Mother Mountain" in the old language. It was almost "Godmother Mountain." Goldilocks felt that this name would increase the Fairy Godmother's enthusiasm for the project. Goldilocks might later suggest "GottMatterhorn" to name the mountain exactly after its creator.

The asteroid would come close to Sol#3.

In a few days, the asteroid would come close to Sol #3. It had been tricky moving the asteroid from the asteroid belt and staying within her energy budget. Marie had not yet told the computers about the final destinations for her asteroid "mountains". She did not want to alert the Department of Planetary Anthropology about her next Good Deed. The Department would just remind her to "Listen, Learn, and Leave it alone!"

Zorcon was far away and Marie enjoyed her independence. When the asteroid got close enough, she would instruct the computers to carve it up and land the "mountains" for the ski resorts. She had not realized that landing the asteroid safely would be a lot easier if the computers had known its exact destination earlier when they planned its trajectory.

2 The First Law

ive young people hiked along the river path. Hansel led. BC and Gretel followed him. Charley and Emma came last. Things had been exciting lately. Hansel was recounting their recent adventure at Alpine Lake.

The young people hiked along the river path.

"Emma – Do you remember the day when we first met you?" Hansel asked.

"I have an excellent memory," replied Emma.

BC snorted. He was amused when Emma talked funny. Her language was sometimes odd, but she was starting to sound more like a normal girl.

A couple of weeks earlier they had met Emma and had hiked to Alpine Lake with Geppetto, Hansel and Gretel's father. What an adventure!

"Baby Red was so cute!" remembered Gretel. Baby Red was a baby sea beast.

"Well, she'll still grow up and be scary like her mother," commented BC.

"Baby Red was so cute!"

"Nessie was only scary when she thought we might hurt Red," protested Gretel.

Emma looked on as the others recounted their adventure.

"It's a good thing that Queen Cinderella showed up," added Hansel. "Nessie was mad. She was pushing her way into the cave and she was not stopping to ask questions."

"It was awesome when Emma turned her arm into a sword," observed BC.

Emma had turned her arm into a sword.

Everyone stopped. Much had happened in a short time. They hadn't asked Emma about her sword arm.

"Can you do that too?" Hansel asked Charley.

Charley thought for a moment. "Yes, I can," he answered. "I can reshape my body within certain limits. Also, protecting humans is the First Law of Robotics," he explained.

> "A robot may not injure a human being or, through inaction, allow a human being to come to harm."

"What about protecting bears?" asked BC.

"What about protecting bears?"

"Interesting question," Charley smiled, pretending to think it over. He turned to Emma. "Are we supposed to protect bears? They are kind of furry."

BC's eyes got big. Hansel snorted, again.

Emma's red eye blinked and her blue eye blinked. Now that she had been with her friends for a while, she realized that Charley was teasing BC. Still, a question had been asked and she would try to answer it. Emma consulted the Zorcon University Library.

"As Charley said, protecting humans is the First Law," she replied. "The meaning of 'human' has been debated since the beginning of robotics. It is generally accepted that 'human' refers to all sentient beings." There was more to say, but Gretel interrupted her.

"The meaning of 'human' has long been debated."

Gretel asked, "What about other androids? Would you protect Charley?"

Now Charley's red eye blinked and his blue eye blinked. The conversation was getting interesting now.

Emma consulted the library again. "This may be difficult to understand. We need to classify Charley," replied Emma.

"That figures," said Hansel. "My dad says that men don't understand women either."

"It's not that," replied Emma. "Charley *was* an appliance designed to make cookies. Android appliances have many limitations. They need to be connected to our computer network in order to access information and to be more sentient. But they are not as valuable as human beings. They are replaceable. Not much is lost if an android is damaged."

"Not much is lost if an appliance is damaged."

Charley pretended to be hurt, but he was listening closely.

Emma continued. "But Charley is no longer a simple appliance. If he were hurt or destroyed, much experience would be lost. He makes judgements. He qualifies as sentient and independent. So, I would probably protect him."

"Probably," smirked BC.

"I probably feel better already," chuckled Charley.

Emma noticed that she had not fully answered the questions. "According to Zorconian history, there is no such thing as a talking bear. That discrepancy is problematic for establishing precedent. Still, people can be furry or at least have hair. So, having fur has nothing to do with whether androids should protect BC."

"Ahem," commented BC.

"I have observed BC, Mama Bear and Papa Bear," Emma continued. "They are not androids, and they appear to be sentient."

"Appearances aren't everything," joked Hansel.

Gretel poked him.

"I would protect BC because he is my friend."

"I would protect BC because he is my friend," interrupted Charley, "not because of the First Law. It would be the right thing to do."

Emma's red eye blinked and her blue eye blinked.

"Thank you, Charley," said BC. "And I would protect you too."

"In fact, you already did," remembered Gretel.

3 Rogue Asteroids at the Wormhole

"Good Morning, Unum. Good morning, Duo."

The Oversight agents looked up at Grimmicus as he came through the door from the sleeping quarters. Duo was at a table in the starship dining area. Unum was ordering breakfast at a food processing station.

"Good morning, Unum."

The Oversight agents responded almost in unison, "Good morning, Professor." They had declined to tell Grimmicus their first names or even their correct surnames. Using his imagination Grimmicus gave them Latin numbers as nicknames. Smithicus #1 became Unum and Smithicus #2 became Duo. For their part, they pretended that "Professor" was Grimmicus' first name. The arrangement suited everyone. Over the two-week journey to Sol #3, they had established a degree of camaraderie.

"Looks like it's pancakes, again," griped Unum. This was starship humor. The automatic food processors were capable of producing any kind of food that they asked for.

"Looks like it's pancakes again."

"We will be in the Sol System in a few minutes," observed Duo. "Then in a few hours we'll be in orbit around Sol #3."

"A direct route then?" asked Grimmicus. "Unless you have surveillance stations in orbit, there should be no orbiting bodies."

"Classified," mumbled Duo.

"Silly," added Grimmicus. "If anyone besides us had observation stations in orbit, that would be evidence of an alien presence on Sol #3. But then we would not come here alone in a simple transport starship, which we are. Ergo, there are no orbiting alien stations."

Unum smiled. "Given your deductive abilities, Professor, we are being silly. We err towards caution. But since you have level #3 security clearance," he added eying Duo, "you are correct. We expect no objects or space debris in our path. We have a direct route to Sol #3 and the high hills of Oberland Kingdom."

Just then a synthesized woman's voice announced, "We will be exiting the wormhole to the Sol system in two minutes. Please secure yourself."

"We have encountered unexpected asteroids."

Grimmicus seated himself and looked at a view screen. There was the usual radiation and distortion near the end of the wormhole.

Suddenly the ship rocked. A crashing boom startled everyone. Emergency airlocks swished shut. The announcer spoke again. "Please remain secured. Executing emergency maneuvers." An emergency klaxon sounded in the corridor.

Grimmicus looked to his companions. Duo looked worried. Unum was lost in thought. Consulting a view screen, Unum observed, "We seem to have encountered rogue asteroids."

Grimmicus raised an eyebrow. He said what everyone knew, "I know that the ship was blind and unshielded for a few moments as it entered normal space. But the odds of a collision must be very small."

Unum spoke first. "According to our most recent survey of the area, the odds of a collision on exiting the wormhole are less than one part in 10^{24}."

"What would change the odds?" asked Grimmicus. "An alien trap?"

Duo spoke to the starship's autonomous concierge, "Red alert. Activate defensive weaponry."

"Red Alert."

Ambient lighting in the cabin shifted to red. Duo's "window" turned into a situational display. He pointed to their starship and the cloud of asteroid fragments.

The ship vibrated as generators started. Looking over Duo's shoulder, Grimmicus saw several disruptor beams flicker as they vaporized rocks in the starship's path.

"At point five light speed, even a small rock could do serious damage," noted Duo.

Unum studied another display. "There is a cluster of rocks on the same trajectory as we are. It is heading towards Sol #3."

Grimmicus raised an eyebrow. The rock cluster was not expected.

Unum continued, "A few rocks entered the Sol #3 atmosphere over the last few days and burned up. Some natives may have noticed a meteor shower."

"This heading of rocks to Sol #3 is not natural."

"Odd coincidence," observed Grimmicus. "I don't remember reading anything about this."

Unum shook his head. "No," he said. "It appears that some asteroids were recently pulled from the asteroid belt. They were sent in a boomerang orbit towards Sol #3."

"That is not a natural phenomenon!" exclaimed Duo, forgetting his usual concern about saying too much around Grimmicus.

Grimmicus asked, "What would cause it?"

"Zorconian nanobots moved it. So, apparently 'we' did. Or at least some Zorconian did."

"Are we in danger?" asked Grimmicus.

"We are not in immediate danger," answered Unum. "Our disruptor beams are clearing the area ahead of us. There are some large rocks on our path, but we can navigate around them."

The three men looked to each other, concern on their faces.

"What created this asteroid cluster?" asked Grimmicus.

Unum shook his head. "The cluster started out as a main rock about thirty miles across," he said. "It was accelerated on a fast route to Sol #3 that took it close to the sun. There was ice and nitrogen frozen in the rock. It heated up as it passed close to the sun."

"It exploded!" concluded Grimmicus. Even a planetary anthropologist knew that much about astrophysics.

"What has your student been up to?"

Duo nodded. "Yes. The ice vaporized and exploded the asteroid. Who would arrange this?" he wondered out loud.

Grimmicus had a sinking feeling in his stomach. He shook his head but did not say anything.

"Given the use of our nanobots to move it, this was not done by aliens," commented Duo, questioning his favorite hypothesis.

"Just us," mused Grimmicus.

Unum was thinking along the same lines. "What *has* your student been up to?" he asked.

4 Planet Fall

he Zorconians will be here in a few minutes," announced Elder Coyote.

"You predict their arrival with great confidence."

Mama Bear smiled at him. "I see the light in you, Elder Coyote, Master of the Space and Time Element," she said. "You predict their arrival with great precision and confidence." Elder Coyote responded to the ritual, "I see the light in you, Elder Mama Bear, Master of the Fire Element, and Elder Bear, Master of the Earth Element."

Coyote continued, "The time threads for the next day or so are distinct and clear."

With Coyote's advice, Papa Bear had built a massive table out of wood and stone. The three Elders sat at the table on a hill above Elf Village. Mama Bear's picnic basket rested on the table.

The Elders looked to the sky where meteors had appeared in recent nights.

Meanwhile, in orbit above Sol #3, Unum, Duo, and Grimmicus got ready for their landing drop. Unum spoke, "Starship repairs are complete. We are ready for our trips to the surface. Grimmicus, as our professorial leader, you should go first.

The nanobots assembled a landing craft around Grimmicus.

Grimmicus walked to the landing circle. He sat on a chair at its center. A shimmering swarm of red nanobots assembled a landing craft around Grimmicus. Moments later the landing craft was ready. The ship's iris opened, and the landing craft dropped into space.

The iris opened, and the landing craft dropped into space.

The disk of the starship disappeared in the distance. Grimmicus' landing craft shot across the dark sky towards Oberland Kingdom.

Moments later, Unum and Duo took their turns in the landing circle.

The three landing crafts landed on a mountain meadow above Elf Village in Oberland Kingdom. The Zorconians stretched as they got out of their landing crafts. The fresh air was invigorating after their tense journey from the wormhole and their descent from the starship.

Three Elders watched them from the edge of the forest.

Grimmicus' ship flew towards Oberland Kingdom.

Grimmicus adjusted his bow tie. The two Smiths wore white overalls.

"We should change our clothing to blend in with the natives," suggested Duo.

Grimmicus nodded. Then he smiled, "I will ride a horse. You two can follow on foot, dressed as squires."

Duo missed the jab. "Making a robotic horse could be problematic. What is a squire?"

Unum smiled and answered, "A squire is a kind of servant. But what rank would you assume, Professor, to merit *two* fine servants?"

"We should change our clothing to blend with the natives."

Grimmicus pondered. He had not thought this through.

"Perhaps you should lose the bow tie," suggested Duo. "It does not look like a medieval garment."

"I shall wear a leather vest," offered Grimmicus, still joking. "And you both can wear short pants."

Just then there was a rumbling sound, almost a growl. Papa Bear was laughing at the three men and their silly discussion.

Duo startled and said, "Blast it! I thought we were alone!"

In that moment, several unplanned and accidental things happened. The landing craft were still in Red Alert mode with their weaponry activated. Their artificial intelligence systems did not recognize the three "animals" as sentient. They thought that Papa Bear's deep laugh was a growl. The command language processor interpreted "Blast it!" as a command to disintegrate Papa Bear. The weapon systems targeted the animals with disruptor beams.

Unum gasped when he heard the sudden electric whine as the weapons charged. The landing crafts fired disruptor beams at the three Elders.

The landing crafts fired disrupter beams at the three Elders.

The landing craft's artificial intelligence had not considered several factors. First, Elders including bear and coyote Elders are sentient. They should not be harmed. Second, Elders have strong Elemental training. Firing energy weapons at Elders does not do much. Third, it is especially pointless to fire energy weapons at a master of the Fire Element, like Mama Bear, or at her family and friends.

On reflex, Mama Bear created a protection shield around herself and the other Elders. It blocked and neutralized the disruptor beams. She also channeled a little of the beam energy to warm the pies in her picnic basket.

Elder Coyote howled at the foolishness of the Zorconians.

Elder Coyote laughed, jumped on the table, and howled at the foolishness of the Zorconians.

Papa Bear was less amused.

"Halt!" commanded Papa Bear in his deep Elder voice. Time froze across Sol #3 outside of their protection shield.

Looking back and forth between Mama Bear and Coyote, he asked, "What should we do about these Zorconians and their dangerous machines?"

Mama Bear sighed. "We should pretend that nothing important happened. I will carry the pies down to our visitors. Perhaps you could carry down the picnic table."

The massive stone and wood picnic table weighed about a thousand pounds. That weight was no challenge for Papa Bear. He knew that carrying the massive table would reveal his enormous strength to the Zorconians. He smiled and picked up the table with one paw.

Then he remembered that a bear showing teeth might be frightening for the Zorconians. That made him smile even more.

Papa Bear carried the massive table with a single paw.

Elder Coyote transformed into his human form. He had decided that it might be calming to have a human in their group.

Using the old language, Papa Bear commanded, "Resume."

Time restarted on Sol #3. The three Elders walked down to the watching Zorconians.

5 First Contact

he Zorconians jumped when their energy weapons discharged. The smell of ozone filled the air.

"Firing disruptors is hardly peaceful."

"Cancel Red Alert," commanded Duo, belatedly. It was the first sensible thing he had said in an hour.

Unum and Duo looked at each other.

"What have we done?" asked Duo.

"Among other things," grimaced Grimmicus, "we have lost the opportunity for a discrete arrival and a peaceful first contact. Firing disruptors is hardly peaceful."

Unum drew a wand from his belt. Speaking to the wand, he said, "Play back what happened in the area by the forest. Start a few seconds before the weapons fired."

Unum's wand replayed the previous moments. A caption on the scene said, "Integrating views from all active cameras."

The image showed two bears and a coyote sitting at a massive stone and wooden plank table. The bears wore clothing and were talking as they looked at the landing crafts below. A covered picnic basket sat on the table.

Then there was a bright flash as the disruptors fired. The air sizzled on the path towards the animals, but a yellow shield surrounding them stopped the beams abruptly. The video then showed Papa Bear saying, "Halt!" in his deep voice. A note appeared below the video saying, "temporal gap in the recording."

"Pause the video," said Unum.

"What just happened?" asked Grimmicus.

Duo and Unum looked at each other. "I don't understand this. No technology of ours could block a disruptor beam," said Unum. "Nor do we have any technology that can interrupt time."

"This temporal discontinuity was not an isolated glitch in our systems," he continued. "We have observed other temporal anomalies in events on Sol #3. Things happen here that we cannot observe directly."

"Folk tales!" muttered Grimmicus.

"Maybe not," answered Duo. "This evidence supports our hypothesis that a very advanced alien civilization has arrived here before us," he said.

Grimmicus looked puzzled but nodded. The Oversight agents could be ridiculous or ignorant, but they were logical.

"Resume video," commanded Unum to his wand.

In the moments after the temporal gap, the wand had shown the animals standing. Mama Bear held the picnic basket. Now, the coyote was gone, but a man with wearing clothing of similar coloring stood where he had been.

"So, what is our cover story now?" asked Duo. He suggested, "Do we say 'Greetings, natives! We are from the stars. We come in peace!'"

Unum glared at Duo. Grimmicus smiled and rolled his eyes. They found Duo's suggestion ridiculous.

"Greetings, natives! We come in peace!"

Duo's eyes widened. Speaking softly to his fellow Zorconians, he said, "That very large bear just lifted the table easily. It must weigh eight hundred pounds!"

"Approximately nine hundred and eighty-one point six pounds, assuming typical rock density," calculated Unum. When he was rattled, he sometimes forgot that speaking with high precision numbers made him sound like an android.

Grimmicus looked to his fellow Zorconians. "Oh, my. Just before we left the spaceport, I *thought* that I saw a coyote. I dismissed it as an illusion. Now I wonder."

Just then the ground shook and they heard a thump. The Zorconians looked up from their discussion. The three "animals" had arrived. They were standing a few feet away.

"Gentlemen, would you care for some pie?"

"Gentlemen," said Mama Bear sweetly. "Welcome to Oberland Kingdom. Perhaps you are hungry from your journey. Would you care for some tea and pie?"

6 Qualifying Test

inderwan waved her mermaid tail slowly back and forth, holding her position in the water current.

"Your Water Element training is complete."

The Water Ancient appeared as light and shadow in the depths of the ocean. Over the past months it had changed its appearance from appearing as a sea beast to appearing as a wise old woman. Two eyes glowed faintly.

The Ancient spoke again. "Cinderwan. Only a day has passed outside in Oberland Kingdom, but your year of training in the Water Element is now complete."

"You have healed sea life and you have sealed fissures in the planet's crust. You have grown in compassion and discernment. You have grown as you have embraced the Water Element.'"

Cinderwan bowed. It was important to listen carefully to an Ancient.

Cinderwan remembered the day of the cookie disaster when she had seen Sage heal the forest and meadow. With Elder Thistle as her training guide, she had practiced many healings in the ocean.

"Always make time to meditate, Cinderwan. If you worry too much, call on the Water Element and calm yourself. Pay attention to your heart and call on your wisdom."

Cinderwan nodded. The Ancient was reviewing foundational teachings of the Water Element.

"When water is in balance, there can be joyous acceptance of a fluid situation. There is abundance. But remember, Cinderwan, mind your balance. Joy and calmness can bring clarity and strength, but too much water will dilute your sense of purpose."

As the Ancient spoke, her face began to shift. Bodiwan now faced her.

"Mother," she bowed.

"I am so proud of you, Cinderwan," whispered Bodiwan. She smiled and then she faded. The quiet of the ocean depths returned.

Cinderwan heard a whale singing softly. She turned and saw Thistle in her whale form.

"I see the light in you, Elder Thistle of the Water Element," murmured Cinderwan in the ritual.

"Your Air Element training will soon begin."

"I see the light in you, Elder Cinderwan of the Earth, Fire, and Water Elements," sang back Thistle. She continued, "Change is coming. Soon you will begin training in the Air Element."

As the whale spoke, Cinderwan heard the roar of water and air rushing from above. She looked up. The swirling vortex of a tornado surrounded her and lifted her up to the sky.

Moments later Cinderwan looked down from the clouds. A whale jumped gracefully from the sea and dove back to the ocean. The water was already calming.

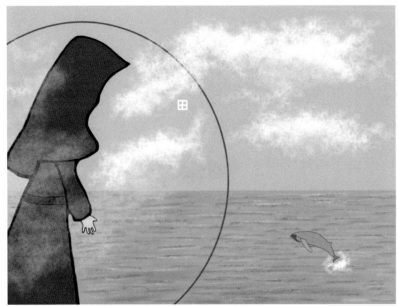

A whale jumped playfully from the sea.

Invoking her Water and Earth training, Cinderwan calmed herself. She surrounded herself with a protective shield of ice. The wind blew her across the sea towards a desert. A sandstorm raged below. The wind shifted and slammed Cinderwan's ice shield down to the desert sand.

The sandstorm intensified. Particles of sand blasted the ice and began wearing it away. The ice ball would not last for long. Cinderwan focused her Earth Magic. She surrounded herself with a rock wall.

The wind intensified. The sand in the air began to erode the rock.

Cinderwan puzzled. She asked herself, "What lives in the desert and is *not* harmed by the wind?" She smiled and reshaped herself as tumbleweed.

Air is the element of rapid change, Cinderwan.

Immediately the wind lifted her up and tossed her around. The tumbleweed bounced on the sand. It yielded to the force of the wind. The wind's howling increased. The wind blew Cinderwan against cliffs and across the desert.

Hours went by. The wind did not slow. Cinderwan closed her eyes. She asked for wisdom.

Faintly at first, she heard Bodiwan whisper, "Air is the Element of change, Cinderwan. Air Magic can transform the negative to the positive, hate into love, and pride into peace."

Cinderwan puzzled. "Mother, I have adapted myself to the wind. It keeps blowing."

Bodiwan breathed but said nothing.

Cinderwan breathed. The air filled her lungs and refreshed her. Suddenly she understood. Changing her body was not enough. She had to change more. She was not just *in* the universe. She was *part of* the universe. She was the wind. She would change the wind and its rules.

Cinderwan shifted her shape slightly and was blown high into the sky. Below she saw the workings of the sandstorm. The heat of the sun reflected off the sand and dried the forest. A raging forest fire blasted the land. The blaze pulled more wind in from the desert.

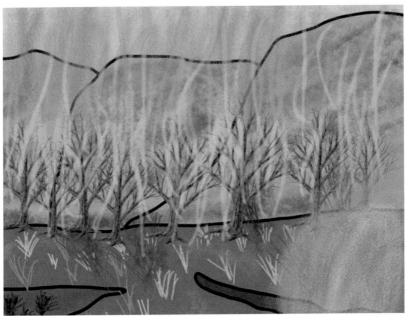

The trees by the dry mountains were burning.

Cinderwan smiled. She knew what she had to do. Using her Fire Magic, she pulled heat out of the desert and cooled the sand. Using her Water Magic, she formed rain clouds in the sky and blocked out the sun. Using her Earth Magic, she made channels in the desert for a river and small streams. Rainwater filled the river. Its banks turned to mud. Healing with her Water Magic, she encouraged plants to sprout along the river.

The wind died down. The rains put out the fire. Plants grew and spread. Below her now was a green valley where before there had been only desert.

Cinderwan dropped down from the sky and returned to her human form. She heard a flutter of wings and then music of a flute. Cinderwan turned. An Indian dressed in leathers sat playing a flute.

Cinderwan called out, "I see the light in you, Elder Eagle of the Air Element."

"That was a breeze."

Elder Eagle stopped playing. He bowed and returned the ritual greeting. "I see the Light in you, Elder Cinderwan of the Earth, Fire, and Water Elements."

They faced each other. Cinderwan smiled at her old friend, Elder Eagle.

"That was a breeze," joked Cinderwan. She grinned slyly as she hid behind her double meaning.

"No small breeze," replied Elder Eagle.

Then he said, "Congratulations, Cinderwan. You have passed Moriah's qualifying test. The Air Ancient finds you worthy of training."

Cinderwan bowed and said, "I am honored."

Elder Eagle continued, "Many who would be Air Elders fail to grasp the meaning and purpose of Air Magic. Moriah will determine your training. I am here to observe and assist as needed."

7 The Piper and the Children

mma and Charlie caught up with the others at the Troll Bridge.

Emma and Charley caught up with the others.

Emma turned to Charley. "I just noticed a clock mismatch when I synchronized with the Zorcon University Library. Has this ever happened to you, Charley?"

Charley replied, "I don't connect to the University Library these days."

What time do you have?" she asked.

Charley shrugged and sent his clock readings to her wirelessly, since that was the most accurate way. Emma's eyes got big. "Your time mismatch is greater than mine. What could cause these anomalies?"

Charley had some ideas about the anomalies, but he simply said, "Some unusual things happened on my last day as a Cookie Machine."

Hansel overheard the androids talking. He thought back to when Charlie was still the Cookie Machine. He remembered being with Gretel in the Fairy Godmother's cottage and eating cookies. Hansel said, "There were *lots* of cookies that day!"

"There were lots of cookies that day!"

"I could use some cookies now!" grumbled BC.

Just then, the faint sound of pipe music reached everyone's ears. Gretel exclaimed, "What lovely music!"

Hansel smiled. "It is coming from ahead near the Troll's Cave. Let's go see what's happening!"

Immediately, Hansel, Gretel, and BC ran ahead.

In the distance Charley and Emma saw a piper playing. The piper was marching with a group of children towards the Troll Cave. Emma and Charley puzzled and looked at each other. They shrugged, and then ran to catch up with the others.

The piper was marching with a group of children.

Charley remarked, "You may notice time gaps in the cave."

"What do you mean?" asked Emma.

"I have been here before. Inside the cave there is a path to a hidden valley," answered Charley. "My understanding of physics is only rudimentary, but the valley is big. It should not fit inside the cave. Also, the valley is open to the sun but the roof of the cave has no hole. When I compared the positions of the sun inside and outside of the cave, there was about an hour's time difference. I conclude that the sun seen in the cave is not the same sun that we see outside."

Emma consulted her library. "That is a very strange anomaly. Is this cave a portal to a different part of Sol #3?" she asked incredulously.

"I don't know," answered Charley. "It may be stranger than that. Gravity in the cave was lower too.

Emma looked thoughtful. This information did not make sense. She asked, "Why are the others racing to the cave? They seem to have forgotten us!"

"I don't know," answered Charley. "At first I thought that they were hungry for the cookies in the cave, but that doesn't really explain this."

Ahead of them, BC, Hansel, and Gretel reached the piper and entered the cave. The piper looked up as Charley and Emma arrived.

"Our last stragglers," the piper said.

"Come along and join your friends."

"Why is everyone going into the cave?" asked Emma.

"You are interesting ones," remarked the piper, not answering her question. "Come along and join your friends. All will be explained."

Emma looked to Charley. She beamed a message to him wirelessly. "The pipe player seems to have hypnotic control over the children. Everyone is acting strangely. I am concerned."

"The way to the Hidden Valley is through the falls."

She reminded Charley, "A robot may not injure a human being or, through inaction, allow a human being to come to harm. Under the First Law, we may need to protect the children from the piper."

"The First Law crossed my mind, too," replied Charley. "Let's follow them and see if we need to do something."

Charley and Emma entered the cave. They saw BC disappearing into the waterfalls as they walked across the troll's kitchen.

Charley turned to Emma and explained, "The way to the Hidden Valley is through the falls". The androids looked at each other and stepped into the mist.

8 Sun Storms on Zorcon

orgive my manners," said Mama Bear nodding to the Zorconians. "Let me introduce myself. Everyone calls me Mama Bear."

"Everyone here calls me Professor."

The Zorconians stared at her, speechless.

Grinning, Mama Bear continued, "I also answer to that name."

"Very logical," remarked Grimmicus at last. Looking to the two Oversight agents, he continued. "I am Johanicus Grimmicus, but everyone here calls me Professor."

He bowed and shook Mama Bear's paw, which was more like a hand than he had expected.

"These are my two colleagues," he continued. "Unum Smithicus and Duo Smithicus."

The Oversight agents bowed.

"Are you brothers?" asked Mama Bear.

The agents looked at each other, puzzled.

Papa Bear explained, "You have the same last name."

"I am called Papa Bear."

The Smiths looked at each other, raising their eyebrows. It was Oversight policy for agents to give their name as "Smithicus." Instead of striking fear as usual, the policy made them look silly here.

Papa Bear turned to Unum and said, "But you are rather different." Unum was not sure how to interpret Papa Bear's comment. Could the bear see inside him? Neither Grimmicus nor Duo knew that Unum was made largely of titanium.

"And you are named with Latin numbers," added Mama Bear, "as if you were son #1 and son #2."

"This is our friend, Coyote."

Unum and Duo were speechless.

Unum turned to Papa Bear and answered Mama Bear's question, saying, "It's more of a coincidence. And you sir, what are you called?"

"I am called Papa Bear," he replied.

Grimmicus could hardly suppress his mirth. "Of course, you are," was all he managed to say. What would his colleagues think of the situation? He was on a backwards world talking to animals.

Grimmicus remembered seeing recordings of Papa and Mama Bear's cottage from Marie Gottmothercus' wand. Papa Bear turned to the thin man next to him and said, "This is our friend, Coyote."

Duo's eyes got big. Grimmicus realized that the coyote had transformed into the man. There was a lot to learn about Sol #3.

Marie Gottmothercus' ridiculous and implausible reports were quite literally true. His reputation would go up in smoke. Behind his back his colleagues might call his reports "Grimmicus' Fairy Tales".

"What are you a professor of?" asked Mama Bear.

Grimmicus started to answer. He puzzled about how to explain "the study of extraterrestrial civilizations". Unexpectedly Duo answered for him. "He is a professor of Planetary Anthropology," he said.

Coyote was mostly invisible when he was on Zorcon.

"I see," said Papa Bear. "You are from Zorcon, on the other side of the worm hole?"

Duo gulped. Could these animals be from the advanced alien civilization that they had worried about? "You know of Zorcon?" he asked.

"I have never been there," answered Papa Bear. He thought it best not to mention that Coyote had recently returned from Zorcon. In any case, Coyote had been mostly invisible during his visit.

"My family has seldom traveled far from Oberland Kingdom," he said. "But I have visited other parts of this world."

"Why don't we all sit down and have some tea and pie," suggested Mama Bear, "so that we can we get to know one another a little better."

"Mama Bear," prompted Grimmicus. "We need to apologize for the disruptor beams fired by our craft. That was accidental. We are relieved that none of you were harmed."

"It was nothing," shrugged Mama Bear.

Mama Bear's response didn't reassure Duo in any way. He looked to Unum. What manner of beings would be unconcerned about a blast from a disrupter?

"Those automated systems need some adjusting," grumbled Papa Bear stiffly.

That comment did not make Duo feel any better either.

"We have a wise scholar at Oberland School," offered Mama Bear. "You might find him interesting," she continued looking to Grimmicus.

"I did not expect to find such learned people here on Sol #3," said Grimmicus.

"We call our planet 'Earth'," interjected Coyote wryly.

Graciously, Grimmicus added, "I feel that I may be at a disadvantage trying to keep up with him!"

Duo had been fiddling with his wand, hoping to record some of the conversation at this first contact. He accidentally pushed a button on it and a news story appeared in the air in front of the group.

"Temperatures are dangerously high across Zorcon."

Scenes appeared of a hot and enlarged sun over a city. A woman newscaster spoke. "Temperatures are dangerously high across Zorcon," she said, "as solar storms continued through the day. Power systems are at maximum capacity. Systems and appliances have been advised to drastically reduce energy demands and to provide only life-essential services."

Duo commanded, "News off."

The Zorconians looked at each other.

Papa Bear growled softly, "The situation on Zorcon sounds serious."

"I am afraid that it is," acknowledged Unum. "Our crisis has been building for some time, but we have been ignoring it."

"Your sun is on the edge of going critical," observed Coyote, without explanation.

"How do you know this?" asked Unum.

Coyote shrugged. "There may be a way to address this," he answered cryptically.

Unum blinked his eyes rapidly. Papa Bear saw that beneath the surface, Unum's right eye had a faint blue glow, and his left eye had a red glow. "I never imagined when we came here that we might ask for your help," commented Unum.

Papa Bear nodded. "Perhaps something will be possible. I am not certain. But first we need to address the problem of the asteroids now heading towards the earth."

Unum sighed. "We Zorconians seem to have made a mess of things," he acknowledged.

"We will need our strength and our rest," commented Mama Bear. "Let us give thanks for what we have. We can talk over pie and tea."

9 Sky Dive

I t was a sunny day for a sleigh ride. Nick called his three reindeer together and hitched them to his flying sleigh. Sage and Nick snuggled as they glided over the snowy landscape. Two yellow beams traced out ahead of them. A trail of red nanobots floated behind in their wake, powering their flight.

The reindeer struggled as the sleigh dropped.

Suddenly the red nanobots faded. The sleigh shuddered and started to fall.

Sage closed her eyes and concentrated. Although Water Magic was her forte, all Elders had rudimentary training in Air Magic. Yellow sparkles surrounded the sleigh. The sleigh's sky dive stopped. Sage smiled and then sent out an Elder Call for assistance. She looked reassuringly at Nick.

"What is happening?" asked Nick.

"The Fairy Godmother's flying magic seems to be faltering," said Sage simply. "I am using a little Elder Magic. We are not in danger."

"My tooth feels numb," commented Nick. "It relies on the Fairy Godmother's magic.

"I can fix your tooth," smiled Sage.

"I can fix your magical tooth."

She explained, "The energies that your tooth requires are within my Water Magic abilities. Right now, though, I would like some help with the Air Magic."

Just then an eagle and a blue hawk appeared on each side of the sleigh. Sage recognized Elder Eagle at once. The blue hawk was unfamiliar.

"It's me, Cinderwan," called out the blue hawk. "Something has gone wrong on Zorcon. Their power is failing."

Moments later, the reindeer felt a lift as Elder Eagle and Cinderwan supported them with Air Magic. Santa's flying sleigh raced ahead towards Oberland Kingdom.

"It's me, Cinderwan."

Cinderwan saw Papa Bear, Mama Bear, and Coyote on a hill below, just above Elf Village.

"Can you see what's happening down there?" she asked Elder Eagle.

Elder Eagle winked and answered her with a question, "Do eagles have sharp eyes?"

Below them were three landing craft, three strangers, and three Elders. Papa Bear waved to them as they descended to the mountain.

As Nick landed the sleigh, Elder Eagle and Cinderwan transformed into their human forms.

Elder Eagle and Cinderwan transformed into their human forms.

The Zorconians watched, intrigued by the arrival of the flying sleigh and its colorful occupants.

Mama Bear bowed slightly to the Zorconians, "Allow me to introduce you to Queen Cinderella, Mr. Eagle, Sage, and Santa Claus. They are dear friends of ours."

"I introduce you to Queen Cinderella, Eagle, Sage, and Santa Claus."

Grimmicus was overcome by it all. He giggled and said again, "Of course, they are!"

10 The Asteroid Crisis

his sleigh is a great ride!" exclaimed Grimmicus.

Everyone was scrunched in the sleigh.

Grimmicus, Unum, and Duo were scrunched together in the back seat of the sleigh, where Santa usually kept his magical bag of Christmas gifts. Santa and Sage were in the front seat.

The Oversight Agents and Grimmicus were curious about the sleigh. They knew that the Fairy Godmother had been involved in creating it.

"The Zorcon power network is offline. How does the sleigh fly?" asked Duo.

Unum shot the younger Oversight agent a glance. When Duo was rattled, he did not keep secrets well. He forgot security protocols and said too much.

Nick was about to say, "Elder Eagle fixed the sleigh for us." Just then,

Sage patted his hand. The pat was a signal that he should not mention Elder magic.

Nick said, "The reindeer are in fine form. We will be at the North Pole in an hour or so."

His answer sounded unconcerned. Duo was relieved that the natives said nothing about the power network. They were silly bumpkins.

"Will you return to Oberland Kingdom to pick up the others?" he asked innocently.

Nick saw the blue hawk and the eagle flying ahead of the sleigh. They would arrive at the North Pole ahead of the sleigh. Elder Coyote might open a direct portal to the North Pole. Again, Sage patted his hand and Nick said nothing.

"Two large asteroids will strike Sol #3 in two days."

Just then a series of beeps sounded on the wands carried by the three Zorconians.

"Power is back online," remarked Duo, stating the obvious. He raised his wand and asked it, "What is happening with the asteroids heading to Sol #3?"

Duo's wand projected an image in the air. A view of Sol #3 from space appeared with a newscaster reporting. She said, "Two large asteroids will strike Sol #3 in two days."

Nick and Sage looked to each other. This sounded bad. It was very bad.

11 Pyramid at the Pole

oyote, Elder Eagle, and Cinderwan stood somberly on a plain at the North Pole. Coyote had his human form but with his coyote head.

"I see the light in you."

"Interesting smile, Elder Coyote," kidded Cinderwan bringing some lightness to the situation.

Coyote remained serious. "Expect the unexpected, Cinderwan. Much depends on you."

He continued, "Crashing the asteroids was not the Fairy Godmother's plan, but she did not plan well. In two days, the asteroids will collide with Earth. One will hit here at the North Pole. The other will hit Oberland Kingdom. The effects will be catastrophic. There will be earthquakes and tidal waves. A cloud of dust will block out the sun for years."

Cinderwan gasped. Unless this catastrophe was averted, many would die.
Elder Eagle nodded and shrugged. He said, "This is your next test."
Cinderwan's eyes widened.

"Moriah works in obscure ways," continued Elder Eagle. "As the time for your dark retreat approaches, this crisis presents itself."

Elder Eagle's answer had an indirect meaning. The Elders would help Cinderwan, but Moriah wanted this challenge.

Elder Eagle explained further, "By tradition, a student is expected to find a suitable cave for a dark retreat. Or the student can build a Meditation Pyramid for a dark retreat. There are no caves near here. You are permitted to use any of your trainings as needed."

As a Space and Time master, Coyote offered his help. "A dark retreat lasts 49 days. We have 49 hours before the asteroids arrive. I can compress time within a Meditation Pyramid. Inside the pyramid, *49 days* will pass. Outside, only *49 hours* will pass. This is the time that you have."

Cinderwan created stone blocks and floated them into place.

Cinderwan understood. She could build a Meditation Pyramid for her dark retreat. During her dark retreat, she should address the asteroid crisis.

Cinderwan focused on the rocky shelf beneath the North Pole plain. Her eyes glowed bright yellow as she concentrated. Rocks rose from the ground. Rocky flakes chipped from their edges, shaping the rocks into large, squared blocks. Cinderwan had the beginnings of Air Element training. Air condensed and expanded under the blocks, lifting them into place. Using Earth Magic, Cinderwan created blocks from the rocks, and then floated them into place.

Next, a stream of molten iron rose from the ground. It formed an iron door on one side of the pyramid. A rain cloud appeared above the pyramid. Rain poured down on the pyramid, cooling the metal.

Cinderwan thought about the gift of life. She smiled and raised her hand again. The rock chips dissolved on the plain and a rich soil surrounded the pyramid. Then a group of trees grew quickly, rising out of the ground around the pyramid.

Elder Eagle's eyes grew wide at Cinderwan's combined use of Earth, Fire, and Water Magic. He turned to Elder Coyote. Coyote shook his head. They had not expected such a masterful display of multiple Elemental Magic.

Cinderwan bowed to them as she prepared to enter the Meditation Pyramid. She wore her pilgrim robe, but she looked different. Her eyes were still glowing yellow.

The pyramid door closed behind her.

"I see the light in you, Elder Eagle of the Air Magic. I see the light in you, Elder Coyote of Space and Time Magic."

Elder Coyote bowed to Cinderwan and continued the ritual. "I see the Bright Light in you, Cinderwan, Master of Three Elements."

Elder Eagle also bowed. "I see the light in you Cinderwan, Master of the Earth, Fire, and Water elements. Your Air Element training continues." He bowed.

Cinderwan adjusted her posture.

The pyramid door opened as Cinderwan approached and closed quietly behind her. It was time to cultivate inner stillness.

Cinderwan settled on a bench and adjusted her posture. She closed her eyes. The room dimmed and became black. She began her dark retreat. How was she expected to save the world from the asteroids? She prayed for guidance.

12 Good Deed Gone Amok

arie frowned at her wand. She had commanded it to sculpt the asteroids into mountains. It should land one mountain at the North Pole and another in Oberland Kingdom. However, her finicky wand reported that the required energy was not available to carry out her commands.

"Earthquakes are expected."

She was worried. She asked her wand to display the predicted path of the asteroids. A picture appeared in the air before her.

"What will happen to the asteroids?" she asked. Marie heard a sound behind her, but her attention was on the wand's display.

"There will be earthquakes at the North Pole and in Oberland Kingdom," said the narrator from the wand. "Tidal waves will hit the coasts. A dust cloud will cover Sol #3 for twenty years, blocking out the sun. An Ice Age will begin."

Just then she heard a familiar voice behind her. Marie paled. It was a voice she had not expected to hear. This was the worst possible moment to hear it. It was Professor Grimmicus.

"Having difficulties with your Good Deed?" he asked, dryly.

Marie spun around. Grimmicus was with two men dressed in white. Off in the distance was a pyramid that she had not noticed before. Behind them on the left she saw Santa's sleigh. Nick and Sage were nearby.

"Having difficulties with your Good Deed?"

"What can you tell us about the asteroids?" asked Duo, without waiting for an introduction.

Marie was thrown off balance. "My wand says that there is not enough energy available to land the asteroids properly. Why is this happening? Somebody needs to fix the power network," she insisted.

"What was your plan?" asked Grimmicus, ignoring her question.

"One asteroid was supposed to make a ski mountain near Santa's workshop for the elves," answered Marie. "The second asteroid was supposed to make a mountain for a ski resort in Oberland Kingdom. Um ..."

Grimmicus nodded. His student was far past following the three L's. She had been much more creative than anyone had expected. She had not been careful.

Unum frowned. He was using his wand to try to arrange a different and less catastrophic outcome. The options were not promising.

"What in heaven's name is that?"

"There is no energy available from Zorcon to alter the course of the asteroids," he announced. "One asteroid will hit here, at the pole. The other will hit Oberland Kingdom. The long-term effects for Sol #3 include an Ice Age. There is nothing we can do to prevent this."

The Zorconians looked at each other as they took in the gravity of the situation.

In that moment, there was a flash and the thunder of energy ripping through the atmosphere. The Zorconians spun around. They had not paid much attention to the pyramid behind them on the North Pole plain. A blue beam shot upwards from the pyramid.

"What in heaven's name is that?" gasped Grimmicus.

"I didn't do it," answered Marie. Nobody was listening to her.

Duo's eyes opened wide.

"Something big is happening," he said.

Unum nodded and said what was beginning to occur to the other Zorconians. "The natives have unimagined resources. Perhaps they can help with our situation on Zorcon."

13 Cinderwan's Dark Retreat

inderwan sat in the pyramid chamber for several hours. She stared into the darkness. She chanted softly to calm her mind as she drifted in and out of a trance. Projecting her mind upwards, she saw two asteroids approaching the earth.

Cinderwan projected her mind upwards.

Images flickered in her imagination. Cinderwan imagined the new mountains. A mountain at the North Pole would cause the planet to wobble on its axis. Sol #3 deserved better. Cinderwan asked for guidance.

She rested in Stillness, Silence, and Spaciousness. Cinderwan asked for guidance.

She asked, "Is this situation right for the Earth, for the proper course of things, and for my people?" Cinderwan waited for clarity.

Cinderwan's question reverberated through Sol #3. The crashing of the asteroid was *not* Earth's destiny. How could the asteroid's path be changed?

Cinderwan pictured the asteroid circling in a stable orbit. How could this be arranged?

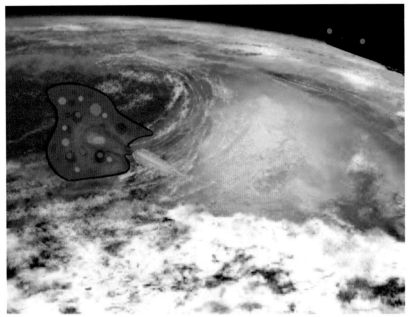

Vaporized lava shot out of the asteroid.

Cinderwan felt the presence of Pele, the Fire Ancient. She remembered a volcano on Hawaii. Could a small volcano on the asteroid rocket it to a better orbit?

"Thank you, Pele. Thank you, Pele!" she whispered.

More of the Ancient's thoughts flowed through her. The Earth, Fire, and Water Ancients were linked together. "We are with you, Cinderwan," they said.

The asteroid cores became superheated. They developed channels. Vaporized lava rocketed out the channels and propelled the asteroids. Over the next few hours, the asteroids moved into stable orbits.

14 Honey in the Breeze

he Zorconians watched the sky and monitored the asteroids. Unum used his wand to project an image of them as recorded by their transport starship. Yellow bursts of vaporized lava shot from each asteroid.

Fire energy is at work.

"Look at this," he said to Grimmicus, Duo and Marie. "The asteroids are shooting plasma like rockets!"

"How could they do this?" asked Grimmicus.

The display indicated that the asteroid cores were superheated. Unum shook his head. What could cause this? The asteroids were moving to a stable orbit.

Duo blinked. "Somebody is rescuing the situation from disaster."

"Are the Glass Slippers involved?" asked Marie. She hoped to get some credit for the improved situation.

In response to her question, a message appeared in the wand display. It said, "No Zorconian energy is detected."

Duo gazed up to the sky searching for the yellow thread of the asteroids moving. Unum observed, "Without a telescope, you wouldn't be able to see them clearly."

In Oberland Kingdom, Papa Bear and Mama Bear gazed skyward from a mountain's edge. A fire trail appeared in the sky.

"I sense Fire energy at work," observed Mama Bear.

Papa Bear laughed softly. "Our youngest Elder is moving the asteroids."

The bears held hands and looked skywards.

Back in the pyramid Cinderwan considered what to do next. She wanted to land the asteroids safely and without adverse effects. Placing a single mountain near the North Pole would cause the Earth to wobble on its axis. However, a *ring* of mountains *could* balance the new mass at the North Pole. She smiled. That plan was better. But could the massive rock be brought down safely?

"Pouring honey in a breeze."

Cinderwan asked again for guidance. An image came to mind from her childhood. She remembered playing in the woods with other children, elves, and young bears. The bears had climbed a tree to get honey from a beehive. One of the bears poked the hive. A sticky stream of honey poured from it. The honey was blown by the wind and slurped by Baby Bear.

Cinderwan smiled. "Pouring honey in a breeze," she whispered.

Hours later, the asteroids cores heated again. A slow stream of golden lava oozed out and was directed downwards.

A stream of lava directed the asteroid downwards.

Like the honey, the lava fell towards the earth. Then the wind split the lava streams along two paths. One golden rope of "honey" flowed towards the North Pole. Another rope flowed towards Oberland Kingdom. Occasional bursts of lightning in the sky superheated the air and kept the lava 'honey' viscous.

In Oberland Kingdom, the stream of hot lava swayed back and forth as it dropped. It piled up and formed a mountain.

The lava formed a mountain in Oberland Kingdom.

"Pouring honey in a breeze," smiled Mama Bear as she watched the honey-colored lava swing back and forth in the wind.

"Fire heats the honey," said Mama Bear, master of the Fire Element.

At the North Pole, a stream of honey wove slowly in a circle. It formed a ring of low mountains.

"Air directs the honey on its path," said Elder Eagle, master of the Air Element from where he stood at the North Pole. "Cinderwan is learning quickly."

"Honey cools the rock," said Papa Bear, master of the Earth Element as he held hands with Mama Bear.

At the North Pole, Sage said, "Water brings life." The Master of the Water Element sat in Santa's sleigh.

"Space and Time Magic training comes next," said Elder Coyote, as he considered Cinderwan's further Elemental training.

In the pyramid, Cinderwan wept with relief.

15 Refuge in Hidden Valley

harley and Emma walked in the cave. As they turned a corner, they met King Jorgan.

"Is everything all right?"

"Ah, my tin man, and a young woman," said the king.

Charley almost said, "Titanium, not tin." Instead, he bowed and said simply, "Your Majesty."

Charley turned to Emma. "Permit me to introduce Emma. She works for the Fairy Godmother."

Emma and King Jorgan bowed to each other. Jorgan said, "My pleasure, young lady. I have heard a little about you. Welcome to our kingdom."

Emma smiled and said, "I am honored, Your Majesty."

Charley looked up to the king and asked, "Your Majesty, is everything all right here? A piper seems to have hypnotized our friends and other young people. He directed them all into this cave."

King Jorgan smiled. "Everything is happening as we intended, Charley. An asteroid is heading towards Oberland Kingdom. We had to move everyone quickly to a safe place. The Hidden Valley will protect them from the asteroid. For their safety, the Piper brought everyone here from the Noble Village, Bear Village, and Elf Village.

The incoming asteroid was news to Charley and Emma. Emma contacted the Zorcon University Library for information. The library reported that the two asteroids heading to Sol #3 had changed their courses. They had moved to stable orbits around Sol #3 and were shrinking in size. They would not crash into Sol #3. No disaster was expected. No further explanation was available.

Emma bowed again to King Jorgan. "The asteroids have moved to stable orbits and appear to be shrinking. No explanation is available yet," she said.

Jorgan looked at her. "Thank you for that information. It is very good news!" he said.

"I have many things to discuss with you," continued the king. "But first I must speak with my father. Please excuse me." He bowed again, turned, and walked back towards the piper.

Charley and Emma looked to each other. Emma asked, "Is the piper the king's father?"

16 The Pied Piper

*M*ama Bear and Sage walked over to Charley and Emma. Mama Bear said, "Would you help us making pies in the cooking tent?"

"Would you help us to make pies?"

Just then, Santa arrived with Unum, Duo, and the Fairy Godmother. Many people walked over to meet Santa and the Zorconians.

In the distance, they saw Cinderwan arriving with Coyote. Most of the elves accompanied her from the North Pole. They waved to the people of the kingdom. There was much cheering.

King Jorgan and Queen Cinderella waved. The Squire called out that the king had important announcements. After a few moments, people quieted down to listen.

"Everyone," said Jorgan, "I have great news. The asteroids have changed their courses and there is no longer any danger."

"There is no longer any danger from the asteroids."

Everyone cheered and clapped.

"In addition," King Jorgan smiled, "Our kingdom has a new mountain on the edge of the Valle d'Aosta." He nodded to Goldilocks and then to the Fairy Godmother. "We will call it 'The Matterhorn.'"

The Fairy Godmother beamed. Grimmicus shuddered. Smithicus #1 blinked. The Sol #3 inhabitants could be quite surprising.

From inside the Hidden Valley, the residents of the kingdom had not seen the events in the sky. In consultation with the Elders, Jorgan and Cinderella decided not to mention her role in stopping the asteroids and making the mountains. It would be better not to mention Elders, magic, or Cinderwan's growing abilities.

"We will call it 'The Matterhorn'."

Again, everyone cheered for the rescue. The Zorconians looked at each other. They still did not understand how the rescue had happened.

Then Mama Bear called out, "We have prepared a feast to celebrate and because everyone is hungry. There are shepherd's pies for dinner and also berry pies for dessert. Dinner is ready. We could use some help delivering the pies to all of the tables."

At that point, Morgan the Piper stepped up. King Morgan was still dressed as a piper. He said, "I can whistle the pies to the tables. Just toss them to me, and I will send them."

Old King Morgan enjoyed showing off a little now and then. He was a master of the Air Element. And so it was that Mama Bear, Charley, and Emma started tossing pies to King Morgan.

To understand what happened next, it helps to remember that Mama is an Elder, and that Charley and Emma are androids. Each of them could move at superhuman speed. A rapid stream of pies flew through the air towards the piper. Everyone watched. Could the piper keep up with the fast stream of pies?

Mama Bear, Charley, and Emma tossed pies to the piper.

Mama winked at Charley and Emma and they picked up the pace. A blizzard of pies raced through the air towards the piper. Still, Morgan the Piper was practiced in his magic. He whistled the pies unerringly to one table after the next.

Soon most of the pies were delivered. The piper's son, King Jorgan, saw an opportunity for some fun.

Innocently, King Jorgan called out to his father, "Hey Dad! Is that a bug on your shoulder?"

King Morgan looked at his shoulder and took his attention off the stream of pies for just an instant. In that instant Mama Bear, Charley and Emma sped up again. The Piper missed one pie, and it plugged up his flute. The whistling stopped. Suddenly, he was covered in pies.

Everyone had been watching with rapt attention. Now they burst into laughter. The piper was covered by the sticky pies and crust. In the gale of merriment, Morgan laughed too!

Hansel exclaimed, "My goodness! The piper has been pied!"

With her penchant for naming people, Gretel announced to everyone, "King Morgan is the Pied Piper!"

"Hey Dad! Is that a bug on your shoulder?"

Everyone laughed again. In good sport, King Jorgan offered to help his dad, and the two kings went to a tent to clean up.

After that, everyone enjoyed the feast. That night there was much partying around a giant bonfire. This was a day to remember. There was cheer and laughter late into the evening. Afterwards everyone retired to their tents in the emergency camp in Hidden Valley.

17 The Crone in the Mirror

 he retreat in the Hidden Valley was finished. After a day of organizing the return of the villagers, King Jorgan and Queen Cinderella were back at their castle by the lake.

"I'll be seeing you soon."

Cinderwan glanced at her mirror as she prepared for a quiet evening with Jorgan. Suddenly, the reflection in the mirror swirled and shifted. It showed an old crone. With her wrinkles and frown, the crone smiled crookedly at Cinderella.

"Hello my pretty. You are the beauty, in this time and place," she cackled.

Cinderwan did not scare easily. She was no longer a child. She had passed Moriah's test and was now a master of four Elements.

She smiled at the crone. Childhood memories flooded her mind. There had been a house in the woods on chicken legs and skulls. She had used her wits and performed difficult tasks for the old crone. She remembered Baba Yaga!

Baba Yaga would need Elder powers to project herself in a mirror. Cinderwan listed the Elders that she knew about. She had not met them all, but there were normally ten Elders on Sol #3, two for each element. That was not counting herself or possibly the Phoenix. Suddenly she pieced it all together. She knew.

"You mention space and time," smiled Cinderwan sweetly. Cinderwan's next training was for Space and Time. Her next teacher would be a Master of Space and Time. Her Elder teacher must be Baba Yaga. Baba Yaga had taught Cinderella in her childhood.

"I am pleased to see you again, Baba Yaga."

The image in the mirror blinked. Baba Yaga had not expected such quick recognition and realization. She had heard that Cinderwan was growing strong. Perhaps her next apprentice would be worthy.

"Yes, we meet again for more training. You are a quick one, dearie. Are you good at riddles?" she asked. "Mastering Space and Time is not easy. Everything changes in time. So many possibilities or suddenly none at all!"

Baba Yaga blinked, and then continued. "There will be two babies, young Elder. Which one will you save? Yes! That is your riddle. So many consequences. Not easy to choose!"

Cinderwan blinked. She was expecting. Tonight, she would tell Jorgan about their baby. What did Baba Yaga mean with her question 'which baby will you save?' The crone's face in the mirror vanished and Cinderwan saw her own reflection again.

Just then, Jorgan entered the room. "I heard you talking," said Jorgan. "Is everything all right?"

Cinderwan smiled at her husband, the King. "Yes, my dear," she said. "My next teacher paid me a visit. She gave me a riddle. You and I have things to discuss. Let us warm ourselves by the fire."

About the Author

Mark Stefik and his wife, Barbara Stefik, live in northern California. Mark is a computer scientist and inventor. Barbara is a transpersonal psychologist and researcher. They illustrate the stories together.

They can be contacted through their website at www.PortolaPublishing.com

Made in the USA
Middletown, DE
30 April 2021